THE TOWER OF LONDON

THE TOWER OF LONDON

LEONARD EVERETT FISHER

MACMILLAN PUBLISHING COMPANY

NEW YORK

THE ROYAL ARMS

The emblems that appear throughout the book are the Royal Arms of England. From 1066 to 1666, the period covered here, the Royal Arms were redesigned five times. This happened during the reigns of William the Conqueror (1066–1087), Richard I (1189–1199), Edward III (1327–1377), Henry IV (1399–1413), and James I (1603–1625).

The two gold horizontal lions, or *lions passants*, against a red background were the emblem of William the Conqueror. In time, three of these gold lions came to symbolize England itself. The gold floral pattern, or *fleurs-de-lis*, against a blue background signified Edward III's claim to the throne of France. The inclusion of the harp and the vertical lion, or *lion rampant*, in the arms of James I indicated his rule over the kingdoms of Ireland and Scotland.

SITE OF DRAWBRIDGE

THE THAMES RIVER

SITE OF LION TOWER AND ZOO

With appreciation to Dr. J. Malcolm Bean, Professor of History, Columbia University

Macmillan Publishing Company, 866 Third Avenue, New York, NY 10022. Collier Macmillan Canada, Inc.

Printed in the United States of America. First Edition   10 9 8 7 6 5 4 3 2 1

The text of this book was set in 14 point Sabon. The black-and-white paintings were rendered in acrylic paints on paper. The coats of arms were prepared as preseparated art on acetate overlays.
LIBRARY OF CONGRESS CATALOGING-IN-PUBLICATION DATA   Fisher, Leonard Everett.   The Tower of London. Summary: Characterizes the Tower and its people during the turbulent years of the forming of the British nation from 1078 through 1666.
1. Tower of London (London, England)—Juvenile literature. 2. London (England)—History—Juvenile literature. 3. London (England)—Buildings, structures, etc.—Juvenile literature. [1. Tower of London (London, England) 2. London (England)—Buildings, structures, etc. 3. Great Britain—History—1066-1687] I. Title.   DA687.T7F57 1987   942.1'2   87-1629   ISBN 0-02-735370-2

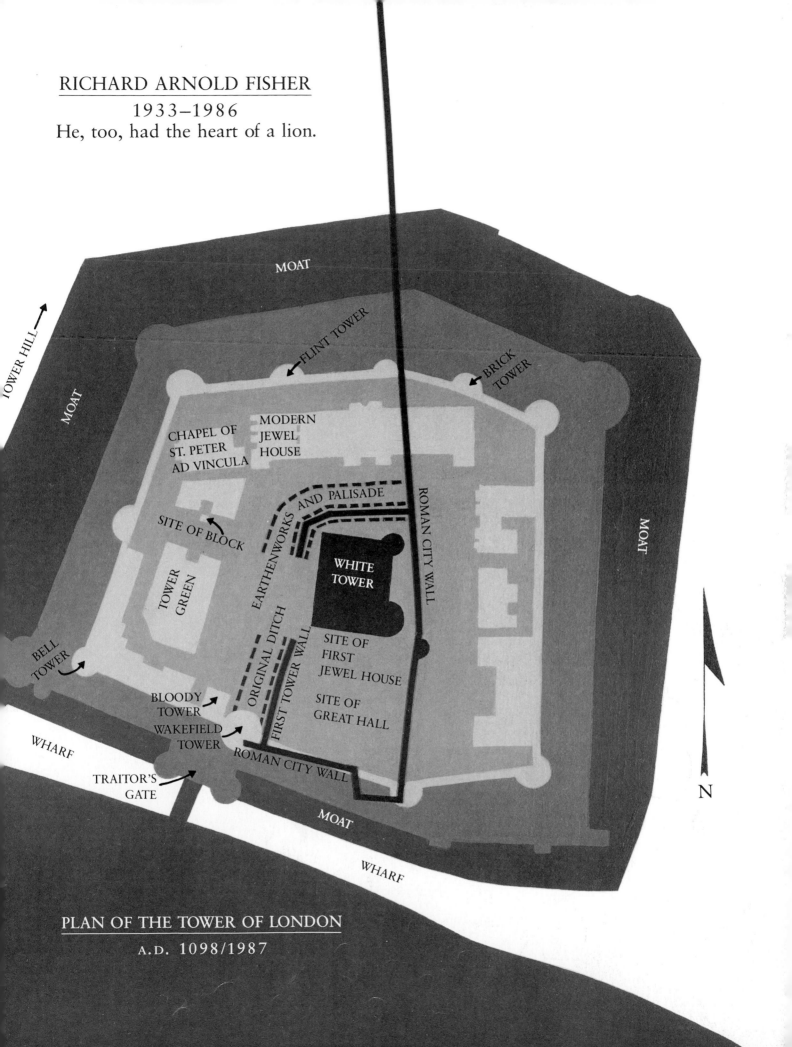

RICHARD ARNOLD FISHER
1933–1986
He, too, had the heart of a lion.

MOAT

TOWER HILL

MOAT

FLINT TOWER

BRICK TOWER

CHAPEL OF
ST. PETER
AD VINCULA

MODERN
JEWEL
HOUSE

MOAT

SITE OF BLOCK

EARTHENWORKS AND PALISADE

ROMAN CITY WALL

WHITE
TOWER

TOWER GREEN

ORIGINAL DITCH

FIRST TOWER WALL

SITE OF
FIRST
JEWEL HOUSE

SITE OF
GREAT HALL

BELL
TOWER

BLOODY
TOWER
WAKEFIELD
TOWER

ROMAN CITY WALL

N

WHARF

TRAITOR'S
GATE

MOAT

WHARF

PLAN OF THE TOWER OF LONDON
A.D. 1098/1987

The Tower of London was begun by a man who was not even English. He was William of Normandy, cousin of England's King Edward. Edward had once promised his throne to William. But, on his deathbed, he gave it to his English brother-in-law, Harold.

William was enraged. He sailed his army across the English Channel to conquer England. On October 14, 1066, he met Harold at Hastings and crushed him. And, on Christmas Day, William—now William the Conqueror—was crowned King of England in the one-thousand-year-old city of London.

William built forts everywhere in his realm. One stood in the southeastern corner of London, near an old Roman wall on the north bank of the Thames River. In 1078, William ordered that the fort be removed and replaced by a great stone stronghold. It was to be a symbol of his power, a fortress for his defense, and a prison for his enemies. It was to become the Tower of London.

The Tower was finished twenty years later, during the reign of William's third son, William Rufus. It rose nearly one hundred feet. Its walls were fifteen feet thick in places. Within them were a chapel, apartments, guardrooms, and crypts. The Tower was protected by a wide ditch, a new stone wall, the old Roman wall, and the river— one on each side. Surely this was a prison from which no one could escape.

The Tower's first important prisoner was the fat and greedy Rannulf Flambard, the unpopular Bishop of Durham. He was dragged there with his servants and bags of money by Rufus's brother, King Henry I. Henry wanted him to suffer. But Flambard lived well in the Tower, bribing his captors with gold. One night in February, 1101, he gave a banquet. When the guards were too drunk to care, he pushed his bulk through a window and slid down a rope to freedom.

The Tower was a fortress-prison until Henry III decided to make it his home. Henry whitewashed the Tower in 1240. He widened the grounds to include a church, a great hall, and other buildings. He called the entire area, now ringed by a wide, water-filled ditch and a thick stone wall with small towers, the Tower of London. And he renamed the Tower the White Tower.

Although it was still a fortress-prison, Henry had turned the White Tower into a dazzling royal palace. Here he entertained important visitors. Most came with gifts. Among these were three leopards, a polar bear, and an elephant. In the Lion Tower, near the drawbridge, Henry built a zoo so that visitors would be greeted by roaring beasts.

By 1377, when ten-year-old Richard II became king, the Tower of London was spread out behind double stone walls and a moat. It seemed completely safe. But on June 14, 1381, a group of overtaxed farmers, led by Wat Tyler, stormed the Tower. Richard and his brothers were safely hidden. However, Tyler found the Archbishop of Canterbury, the Royal Treasurer, a tax official, and a doctor. He had the four men taken beyond the Tower walls to Tower Hill, where their heads were chopped off.

Later Richard made peace with his farmers. But Wat Tyler was beheaded for leading the revolt. As for his own fate, Richard was eventually thrown into a Tower dungeon, where he was forced to give up the throne to Henry IV.

Several monarchs died in the Tower of London. Among them was thirteen-year-old King Edward V. When his father, Edward IV, died, his uncle Richard, Duke of Gloucester, plotted to take the throne for himself. Richard had the king and his younger brother, the Duke of York, taken to the Tower. Lord Hastings, a royal official, tried to protect them. His head was lopped off on the Tower Green. Edward and his brother were murdered, probably in the Garden Tower, which was later called the Bloody Tower. Richard was now King Richard III.

After the death of Henry VII, the Tower of London was never again home to an English king or queen. However, its dungeons continued to hold the reigning monarch's enemies. And the Tower remained the site of colorful celebrations.

One such event was held in honor of the marriage of King Henry VIII to his second wife, Anne Boleyn. On May 19, 1533, the new queen led a great boat parade up the Thames River to the Tower. For the next eleven days the Tower was a place of noisy celebration, highlighted each night by an enormous feast.

The Tower of London was not always a place where Anne Boleyn celebrated. On May 19, 1536, exactly three years after she had first entered the Tower for her wedding party, Henry had her taken to the Tower Green. There Queen Anne laid her blindfolded head on the block and, a few minutes before noon, lost it under a sword.

Anne Boleyn had been accused of misconduct. Her real crime had been producing a daughter rather than a son, a future king of England. Twenty-two years later, however, her daughter became the ruler of England. She was Queen Elizabeth I.

Just as it had her mother, the Tower held Elizabeth prisoner. She had been put in the Bell Tower by her half sister, Queen Mary. Mary felt that her throne was being threatened by several persons, including Elizabeth. She had them all imprisoned in the Tower. But Elizabeth was innocent, and the people knew it. Because of a public outcry, she was released after two months, on May 19, 1554—the anniversary of her mother's marriage celebration and death.

In 1558, Elizabeth became queen. Since it was her duty to "take possession" of the Tower, the symbol of royal power, she spent three days there before her coronation. On January 15, 1559, she left in a glittering parade to be crowned at Westminster Abbey. She never returned to the Tower.

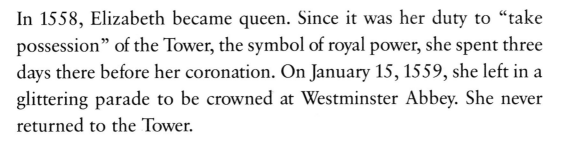

If the Tower held Elizabeth only briefly, it was prison for a long time to her beloved Sir Walter Raleigh, one of her greatest sea captains and soldiers. When Raleigh married, the jealous Queen Elizabeth had him delivered to the Tower through Traitor's Gate. She kept him in the Brick Tower during the late summer of 1592.

After Elizabeth's death, her cousin, King James I, charged Raleigh with treason. Raleigh was innocent. But he was again arrested and taken to the Tower through Traitor's Gate. With his wife and sons, Raleigh spent twelve years in the Bloody Tower, where he wrote *The History of the World*. At the end of that time, King James ordered him to find gold in South America. The expedition was a failure. When Raleigh returned, James had him sent once more through Traitor's Gate. On October 29, 1618, an axman whacked off his head.

Part of the Tower of London became a museum in 1603. Shortly after his coronation, King James I had ordered that the royal jewels be kept in the Tower Jewel House and put on display for Tower visitors.

James was a very unpopular king. He thought God had put him on the throne to have absolute power over England. He was responsible for driving the Pilgrims and Puritans to America, where an English colony, Jamestown, Virginia, already had been named for him. James was also a man who lived beyond his means. To his credit, though, a new edition of the Bible was published during his reign. It was the King James Version.

It was inevitable that someone try to rid England of James I—and end up in the Tower. Guy Fawkes and a band of rebels planned to blow up the king and the Houses of Parliament on November 5, 1605. The Gunpowder Plot failed. The rebels were either shot or captured. Guy Fawkes was flung into Little Ease, a Flint Tower dungeon that was dark, filthy, and so small that a prisoner could hardly sit, stand, or lie down there. Fawkes was stretched on the rack and then hanged.

It was many years before the Tower of London was used as something other than a symbol of royal power, a fortress for the monarch, or a prison for the monarch's enemies. After the reign of James's son, Charles I, who was ordered executed by Parliament, England spent eleven years without a king or queen. During this time, the people endured the harsh rule of Oliver Cromwell.

Finally, in 1660, Parliament put a king back on the throne. He was Charles II, "the Merry Monarch," and it was he who used the Tower of London differently. When the Great Fire swept London from September 2–7, 1666, Charles II opened the gates of the Tower to his burned, hungry, and homeless people.

MORE ABOUT THE TOWER OF LONDON

The Tower still stands. It has been governed by a Constable ever since Geoffrey de Mandeville was appointed the first one nearly nine hundred years ago. Many of the objects that mark the Tower's long and tumultuous history, such as an executioner's ax, armor, and the Royal Arms can still be seen. Among these are the ravens, which link England's past with her destiny. Six of the large black birds are always within the Tower walls. They are cared for by one of the Yeoman Warders, the Yeoman Ravenmaster. The legend about them is at least three hundred years old. It says that when the last raven has left the Tower of London, the British nation will disappear.